FRUITS

by Robin Nelson

first step nonfiction

Lerner Publications Company · Minneapolis

We need to eat many
different foods to stay **healthy**.

We need to eat foods in
the **fruit** group.

Fruits are parts of plants.

Fruits give us **vitamins**
and **minerals**.

Fruits help keep us from getting sick.

Fruits help us grow.

We need two **servings** of
fruit each day.

We can eat an apple.

We can eat kiwi.

We can eat watermelon.

We can eat blueberries.

We can eat strawberries.

We can eat grapes.

We can eat pears.

We can drink orange juice.

Fruit keeps me healthy.

Fats, Oils, and Sweets
Use Sparingly

Milk, Yogurt, and Cheese Group
2-3 Servings

Vegetable Group
3-5 Servings

Meat, Poultry, Fish, Dry Beans, Eggs, and Nuts Group
2-3 Servings

Fruit Group
2-4 Servings

Bread, Cereal, Rice, and Pasta Group
6-11 Servings

Fruit Group

The food pyramid shows us how many servings of different foods we should eat every day. The fruit group is on the second level of the food pyramid. You need 2-4 servings of fruit every day. You could eat a banana, apple, or orange. You could eat a cup of canned fruit. You could drink a cup of fruit juice. Fruits give you vitamins to help you grow. Eating citrus fruits, like oranges and grapefruit, can help your body fight diseases.

Fruit Facts

 Fruit grows on trees, bushes, or vines.

 Fruits have one or more seeds inside of them.

 Citrus fruits contain vitamin C. Vitamin C helps your skin to heal.

 Only fruit juices that are 100% juice can count as a serving of fruit. Many fruit "juices" are mostly sugar and only a little fruit juice.

There are more than 50 different kinds of grapes.

 Strawberries are the most popular berry in America.

 There are 200 tiny seeds on every strawberry.

 Bananas are the most popular fruit in America.

Glossary

 fruit – the part of a plant that has seeds

 healthy – not sick; well

 minerals – parts of food that keep your blood, bones, and teeth healthy

 servings – amounts of food

 vitamins – parts of food that keep your body healthy

Index

apple – 9, 19

blueberries – 12

grapes – 14

kiwi – 10

orange juice – 16

pears – 15

strawberries – 13

watermelon – 11

The photographs in this books are reproduced through the courtesy of: © Todd Strand/Independent Photo Service, front cover, pp. 2, 5, 6, 7, 8, 10, 11, 12, 17, 22 (middle, second from bottom, bottom); © Scott Bauer/ARS/USDA, pp. 3, 14, 16; © Patrick Tregenza/ARS/USDA, p. 4; © Keith Weller/ARS/USDA, pp. 9, 15, 22 (second from top); © Brian Prechtel/ARS/USDA, pp. 13, 22 (top).

Illustration on page 18 by Bill Hauser.

Lerner Publications Company
A division of Lerner Publishing Group
241 First Avenue North
Minneapolis, MN 55401 USA

Website address: www.lernerbooks.com

Library of Congress Cataloging-in-Publication Data

Nelson, Robin, 1971–
    Fruits / by Robin Nelson.
        p.   cm. — (First step nonfiction)
    Summary: An introduction to different fruits and the part they play in a healthy diet.
    ISBN: 0–8225–4624–8 (lib. bdg. : alk. paper)
    1. Fruit—Juvenile literature. {1. Fruit. 2. Nutrition.] I. Title. II. Series.
TX558.F7 N45 2003
641.3'4—dc21   2002013618

Manufactured in the United States of America
1 2 3 4 5 6 – JR – 08 07 06 05 04 03